The Blue Horse:

who wanted to go to college!

By:

Dr. Jose Arturo Puga

illustrated by:

Soor-el Puga

AuthorHouse™
1663 Liberty Drive
Bloomington, IN 47403
www.authorhouse.com
Phone: 1 (800) 839-8640

Published by AuthorHouse: 02/23/2018

ISBN: 978-1-5462-2780-9 (sc)
ISBN: 978-1-5462-2782-3 (hc)
ISBN: 978-1-5462-2781-6 (e)

Library of Congress Control Number: 2018901810

Print information available on the last page.

authorHOUSE®

The Blue Horse Who Wanted to go to College is dedicated to my children Arturo, Jocelyn, Hector, and Julian with a special thanks to my wife Nancy J. Puga for her unconditional love. Soor-el & Amy for their encouragement and support. With this book, I tell my children and siblings, there is a blue horse in all of us.

~ Dr. José Arturo Puga

~~~~~~~~~~~~~~~~~~~~~~~~~~~~~~

I would like to dedicate these illustrations to my familia! With a special thanks to my wife Amy and our children Aiden Miguel and Evan Joaquin. A lifelong of gratitude to our parents Hector and Yolanda for their continuous love and support. ¡Muchas gracias! I hope our Blue Horse inspires you to always follow your dreams and to encourage others along your journey to do the same.

~ Soor-el Puga

Once I met a blue horse named Ruben who wanted to go to college.

He hoped to go to a recognized university. Ruben went to his high

school counselor to ask about a college application.

~~~~~~~~~~~~~~~~~~~~~~~~~~~~~~~~~~~~~~

En una ocasión conocí a un caballo azul llamado Rubén, quien quería

ir a la Universidad. Su esperanza era asistir a una Universidad de

renombre. Rubén fue con el consejero para solicitar una aplicación

para ingresar a la universidad.

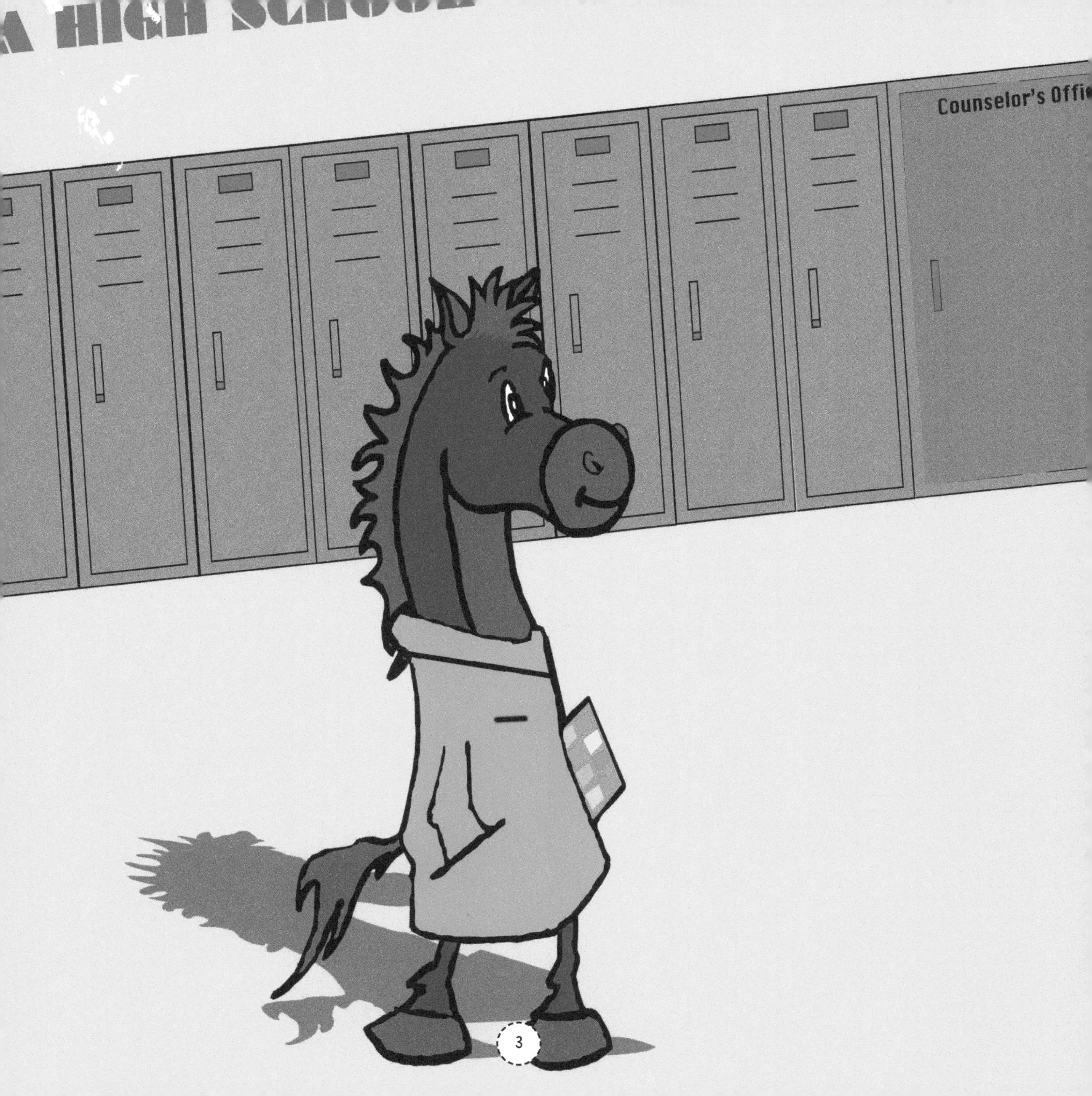
Counselor's Offi

"Mrs. Hayes, I would like an application for college," said Ruben.

She responded firmly, "Don't forget to include all of your grades and the awards you have received in school."

~~~~~~~~~~~~~~~~~~~~~~~~~~~~~~~

"Sra. Hayes, deseo llenar una aplicación de ingreso a la Universidad", dijo Rubén.

Ella respondió con firmeza: "No olvides incluir todas tus calificaciones y los premios que has recibido en la escuela."

Since Ruben knew he had struggled with the English language and his grades, he asked, "What kind of awards should I include, Mrs. Hayes?"

"Well, never mind, Ruben; with your grades, you probably will not be accepted in any of those colleges anyway", Mrs. Hayes quickly responded.

~~~~~~~~~~

Como Rubén sabía que había luchado al aprender inglés y con sus calificaciones, Rubén pregunto: "¿Cuáles premios debería incluir Sra. Hayes?"

"Bueno Rubén, no te preocupes, de todos modos, con tus calificaciones, probablemente, no serás aceptado en esas universidades", rápidamente contestó la Sra. Hayes.

Mrs. Hayes added, "Just complete what you can, and we will send them later. Let's think about other opportunities, like the army; that might suit you just fine."

~~~~~~

La Sra. Hayes añadió: "Completa lo que puedas y la enviaremos más tarde. Vamos a ver otras oportunidades, como por ejemplo, las Fuerzas Armadas, eso te favorece más."

"Let's check your high school graduation plan to make sure you meet the requirements before you start thinking about college or even the army. Well, what do you know? You do meet the requirements for the army. Congratulations, Ruben!" Mrs. Hayes added dryly.

~~~~~~

"Vamos a verificar tu plan de graduación para la preparatoria para estar seguros de que cumples con todos los requisitos antes de comenzar a pensar en la universidad o las Fuerzas Armadas. Bien, ¿sabes qué?, sí cumples con los requisitos para las Fuerzas Armadas. ¡Felicidades Rubén!", añadió la Sra. Hayes en un tono seco.

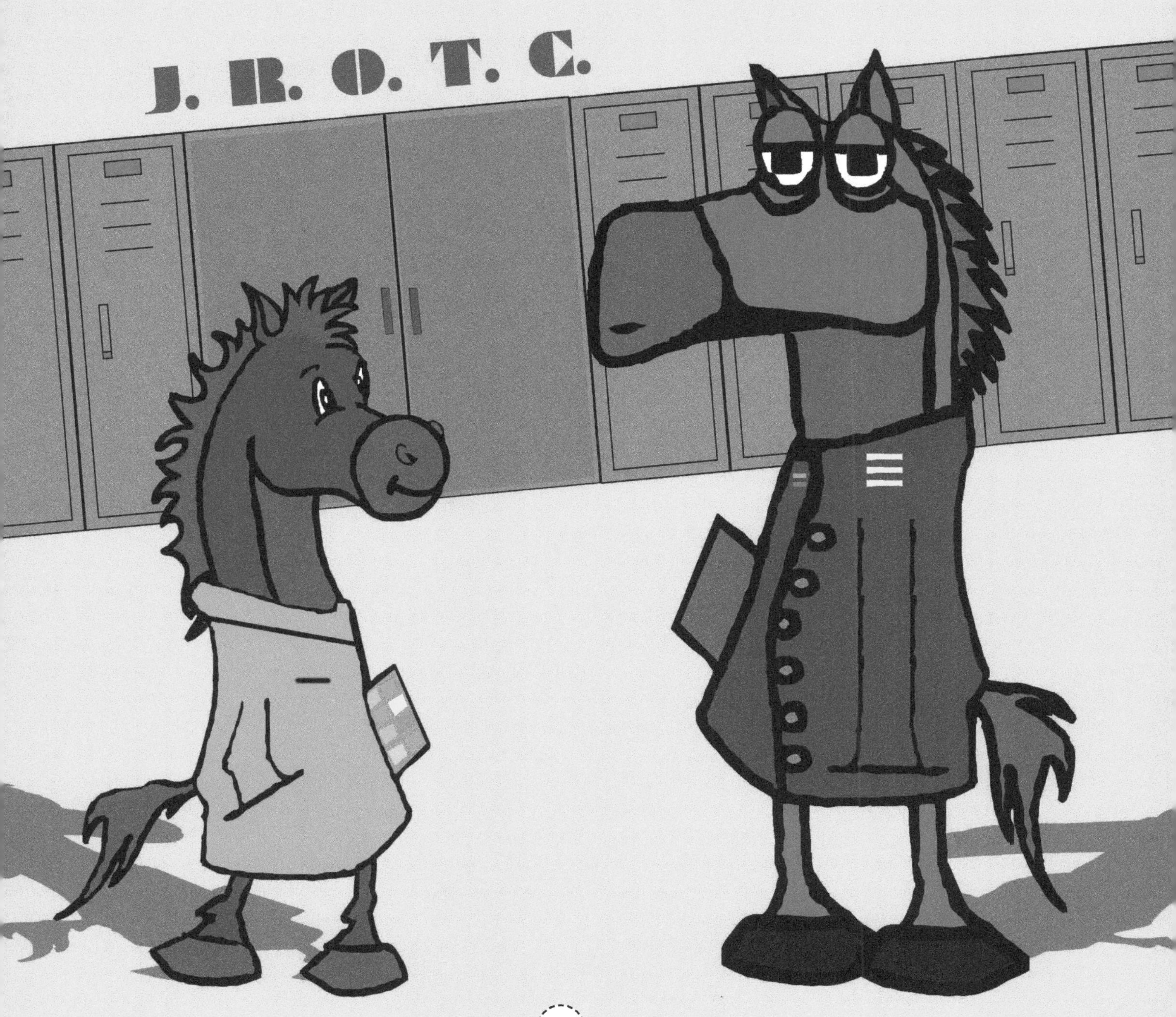
J. R. O. T. C.

The high school graduation date came, and Ruben and his parents were very happy.

"Congratulations!" said his mom and dad.

Ruben replied, "I will go to college and become someone important. I promise you, mom and dad!"

~~~~~~

Llegó el día de la graduación de la preparatoria y Rubén y sus padres estaban muy contentos.

"¡Felicidades!" dijeron su mamá y su papá.

Rubén contestó: "¡Voy a ir a la Universidad y me convertiré en alguien muy importante. Se los prometo, mamá y papá!"

After the graduation, Ruben received a letter from a recognized university, and he was very excited. He could not wait for his mom and dad to open the letter.

~~~~~~

Después de la graduación, Rubén recibió una carta de la Universidad y estaba muy ansioso. No podía esperar que su mamá y su papá abrieran la carta.

Ruben asked his mom nervously, "Mom, would you please open the envelope for me and let me know what the university has to say?"

~~~~~~~~~~~~~~~~~~~~~~~~~~~~~~~~

Rubén le preguntó a su mamá muy nervioso: "Mamá, ¿puede abrir la carta y decirme que dice la universidad?"

Ruben's mom opened the envelope slowly and read, "We appreciate your interest in our university, but we regret to inform you that you are not accepted for the upcoming semester ..."

La mamá de Rubén abrió el sobre y cuidadosamente leyó la carta: "Apreciamos su interés en nuestra Universidad, sin embargo, lamentamos informarle que usted no fue aceptado para el próximo semestre ..."

As Ruben listened, he felt so sad and disappointed. He quietly replied, "Oh well, I'll apply next semester."

His mom said, "Why don't you get a job or take your counselor's advice and sign up for the army?"

~~~~~~

Mientras la madre de Rubén leía la carta, Rubén se sintió triste y decepcionado, y silenciosamente respondió: "Está bien, aplicaré el próximo semestre." Su mamá dijo: ¿Por qué no consigues un empleo o tomas la sugerencia de la consejera y te enlistas en las Fuerzas Armadas?"

Ruben decided not to visit the army recruiter, keeping his dream of going to college alive. Instead, he visited the local library every afternoon to read books. He was determined to go to college.

~~~~~~~~~~~~~~~~~~~~~

Rubén decidió mantener vivo su sueño de ir a la universidad y no visitar las oficinas de las Fuerzas Armadas. En su lugar, él decidió visitar la biblioteca local todas las tardes para leer libros y mantener su determinación de ir a la universidad.

While visiting the library, Ruben asked others about different colleges. He met a library volunteer who was also a blue horse and currently a professor at the local community college.

Mientras visitaba la biblioteca, Rubén preguntó sobre otras universidades y el bibliotecario voluntario que también era un caballo azul, se presentó como el Dr. Stein, quien además era un profesor en el colegio local de la comunidad.

The professor introduced himself and said, "Hi, my name is Dr. Stein. How may I help you?"

Ruben replied, "My name is Ruben, and it is my dream to go to a recognized university."

~~~~~~~~~~~~~~~~~~~~~~~~~~~~~~~

"Hola, me llamo Dr. Stein, ¿cómo te puedo ayudar?", dijo el viejo caballo azul.

Rubén contestó: "Mi nombre es Rubén y mi sueño es ir a una gran universidad."

"Ruben, it is rather simple. First, you need to go to the local community college for a short time, and you must receive good grades. After that, you may apply to the college of your dreams," explained Dr. Stein.

~~~~~~~~~~~~~~~~~~~~~~~~~~~~~~~~

"Rubén es muy sencillo. Primero, tendrás que ir al colegio local de la comunidad por un corto tiempo, mantener buenas calificaciones y a su tiempo podrás aplicar para la universidad de tus sueños.", explicó el Dr. Stein.

Ruben was worried and asked, "How would I be accepted to the local community college?"

Dr. Stein replied, "You do not need to worry. It is an open campus; all you need is a high school diploma."

Preocupado Rubén preguntó: "¿Seré aceptado en el colegio local de la comunidad?"

Dr. Stein le respondió: "Por supuesto, es un colegio de registro libre, todo lo que necesitas es un diploma de escuela superior."

The next day, Ruben went to register at the local community college. After attending for a few semesters and receiving good grades, he applied to a recognized university and awaited a response.

~~~~~~~~~~~~~~~~~~~~~~~~~~~~~~~~~~~~~~

El próximo día, Rubén visitó y se registró en el colegio local de la comunidad. Después de varios semestres y después de recibir buenas calificaciones, Rubén aplicó a la gran universidad y esperó su respuesta.

Ruben had learned the process from Dr. Stein and now wanted to help his friends. He invited his friends Alex, a green horse, and Brianna, an orange horse, to help fulfill their dream of attending college as well.

~~~~~~~~~~~~~~~~~~~~~~~~~~~~

Rubén aprendió el proceso del Dr. Stein y quería ayudar a sus amigos. Decidió invitar a sus amigos Álex, un caballo verde y Brianna, una yegua color naranja, para también ayudarlos a alcanzar su sueño de asistir a la universidad.

A few months later, Ruben received a new letter in the mail. He ran into the house with excitement and said, "Mom and dad, I received my letter in the mail today! Please read it for me."

~~~~~~

Unos meses más tarde, Rubén recibió una nueva carta en el correo. Corrió emocionado y dijo: "¡Mamá y papá, recibí mi contestación hoy en el correo! "Por favor, léamela."

2450

Ruben's mom opened the letter and nervously read, "It is a great pleasure to inform you that you have been accepted into our prominent university, and we would like to extend an invitation to attend our new student orientation ..."

La mamá de Rubén abrió la carta y la leyó ansiosamente: "Es con gran placer que le informamos que usted fue aceptado en nuestra prestigiosa Universidad y deseamos extenderle una invitación para la orientación de nuevos estudiantes ..."

Ruben jumped and wrapped his arms around his mom. He could not contain his excitement! His determination and hard work had paid off. As a result, Ruben, the blue horse who dreamed of going to college, was finally able to fulfill his dream.

~~~~~~

Rubén brincó y fuertemente abrazó a su mamá !No podía contener su emoción! Su determinación y gran esfuerzo valieron la pena. Como resultado, Rubén, el caballo azul, quien soñaba con ir a la Universidad, finalmente pudo realizar su sueño.

About the Author

Dr. José Arturo Puga is a middle school principal at Hays CISD in Kyle, Texas, and a retired US Army officer with twenty-one years of military service. His career in education, which spans more than two decades, includes experience as a bilingual teacher, school counselor, and administrator at the elementary school, middle school, and high school levels.

Dr. José Arturo Puga earned his doctoral degree at Texas A&M University-Kingsville in curriculum and instruction, with a concentration in bilingual education. He earned a bachelor's degree in Spanish literature and a master's degree in school counseling from the University of Texas at Edinburg and at Brownsville. He also earned a master's degree in sociology from Texas Tech University at Lubbock.

Dr. José Arturo Puga, his wife, and their family reside in the Austin area, where he enjoys traveling and spending quality time with his family.

About the Illustrator

Soor-el Puga is the director of Bilingual & ESL Programs at Marble Falls ISD. His career in education, which spans more than seventeen years in central Texas schools and organizations, includes experiences with at-risk youth outreach, the visual arts and elementary classrooms, instructional technology, educational administration, and bilingual education.

Soor-el earned his bachelor's degree from the University of Texas at Austin and master's degree in the arts and education from Texas Tech University. Additionally, he holds an educational leadership certificate from Texas A&M University-Kingsville. Mr. Puga was honored as the Hays CISD Assistant Principal of the Year for the 2013-14 academic year and is also a National Robert Rauschenberg Educational Foundation Award recipient based on his work with special education students in the visual arts.

Soor-el Puga, his wife, and their family reside in the Austin area, where he enjoys new adventures with his family and collecting vintage cameras.

CPSIA information can be obtained
at www.ICGtesting.com
Printed in the USA
BVHW02s1955290518
517560BV00029BA/1656/P